Contents

Chapter 1
I'm Not Creepy

Saturday 25th of June

7.20 p.m.

Matt's Party

The girl was sitting on her own on the sofa.

"Did you just fart?" I asked her. "Because you totally blew me away."

Then I grinned at her. "I'm Joe," I said. "So what's your name?"

The girl didn't tell me. She just leaped up like a salmon and moved away very fast.

She obviously didn't like laughing. Still, there were tons more girls at the party so I wasn't bothered.

7.50 p.m.

I went up to this very pretty girl. "Will you check your pocket?" I said.

"Why?" she asked, and her cute face creased with worry.

I put on a funny voice so she'd know I was joking, and then I said, "Because you've just stolen my heart."

She didn't say anything in reply, and so I gave her a big smile. "I'm Joe," I told her in my normal voice. "What's your name?"

"Got to go to the toilet," she said.

"That's a funny name," I called after her. "And a bit long. Do your friends just call you Toilet for short?"

8.20 p.m.

My big sister Georgia stormed over to me. She was the one who got me the invite to this party. And she didn't look happy.

"What on earth do you think you're doing?" she demanded.

"Only trying to make girls laugh," I said. "Everyone says that's the best way to break the ice. So I found a website with all these brilliant chat-up lines. And to make sure I didn't forget them – I wrote them all on my hands."

"Show me," she snapped.

I showed her. Then she glared at me.

"One word," she said. "Tragic. No wonder everyone thinks you're creepy."

I was shocked. I was horrified. "Who said that?" I asked.

"Every girl you've spoken to tonight," Georgia said. "Joe, go home."

"But it's still early."

She closed her eyes for a minute. "Just go home. Now."

8.35 p.m.

I did as I was told and went home.

I'M NOT CREEPY.

I talk to girls at school all the time. And they like me. Honest they do. Well, Kirsty does. I walk to school with her every day. She says I'm her very best friend. And she trusts me more than anyone.

The trouble is Kirsty's got a boyfriend. So have all the other girls I know. That was why Georgia got me the invite to that party – so I could meet some new girls. Only thing was, not one girl came near me.

So I had to go up to them. And that was
dead hard. For a start, my tongue felt as
if it was stuck down inside my mouth. And
everything I wanted to say got all mixed up.
That was why I thought some funny chat-up
lines might come in handy ...

Only it was a total disaster.

And I haven't got a clue what to do next.

Chapter 2
Hot or Not?

Monday 27th of June

8.45 a.m.

But then I had some brilliant news about Kirsty, the girl I walk to school with. Her boyfriend had dumped her.

Obviously that wasn't great news for Kirsty. At least not at first it wasn't.

When I asked her what had happened,
Kirsty said her boyfriend hadn't been two-
timing her. He'd been THREE-timing her.

"And so," she said, "I hate every single
boy in the whole entire world. Except you, of
course, Joe."

That was my chance, wasn't it?

Kirsty and I get on so well. And now there
was a vacancy. Why shouldn't I move out
of the friend zone and upgrade to being her
boyfriend? I wouldn't two-time her, or three-
time her either.

But I didn't want to rush things. So decided to wait until after school to make my move.

9.20 a.m.

That was the weirdest assembly ever.

Mr Scott, this teacher who thinks he's down with the kids, rocked up to the front of the hall.

And he started talking about dating. We all looked at each other in horror. We couldn't believe it. First, Mr Scott told us how hard it can be to meet someone.

"Is he talking about himself?" Kirsty whispered to me.

Then he told us about online dating.

"That can be risky," he said. "But now," he added with a big grin that showed all his teeth, "there's a 'wicked fresh' scheme called Mate Match."

He told us that on Mate Match you swap first names, pictures and stuff about yourself with pupils from other local schools. Pupils who have never met you. Then you message each other to find out more. And then – if you like the sound of each other – you meet up at Café Pelican for your first date.

Mr Scott was dead excited about it.

He asked anyone who was interested to put their hand up.

"You'd have to be really sad to join that," one boy called out. "Bit like you, sir," he added in a whisper.

And after that not one person raised their hand. Mr Scott wasn't grinning any more. In fact, I thought he was going to cry. But he got himself together and said, "Well, if you like the sound of Mate Match then come and see me later."

I was so glad that I didn't need to bother with that. I had a girlfriend already. Well, I would have after school tonight.

4.00 p.m.

Unbelievable. Totally unbelievable.

Kirsty turned me down!

She was nice about it. "Joe, you are my very best friend," she said. "That's why I can't ever go out with you. You do see that, don't you?"

No. I did NOT see that.

5.35 p.m.

I still didn't get it.

7.20 p.m.

I told Georgia what Kirsty said. I was so fed up and confused that I had to tell someone.

"What in the name of Godzilla is wrong with me?" I asked.

Georgia sat down next to me. "Let me explain," she began. "Boys are either hot or not. And you're *so* not hot."

"That's enough," I muttered, and I gave her a "shut up" look.

But she didn't shut up. Oh no.

"I'm only being honest, Joe," she told me. "Girls like you but they don't fancy you. You're just not hot enough. But ..." She looked at me sideways. "Perhaps you can be hot."

"How?" I asked.

"By a total change of image," she said. "Then you need to meet girls who don't know about your lack of hotness."

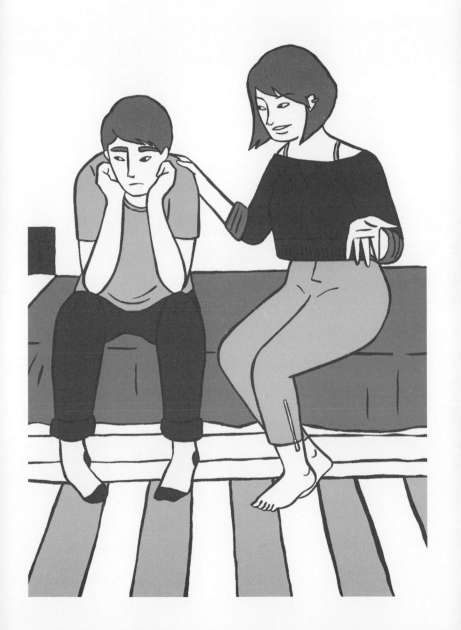

That was when I made a very casual reference to Mate Match. I thought Georgia would scoff at me, but instead she jumped up with excitement.

"That's the perfect way to do it," she said.

"But isn't it a bit sad ..." I began.

"Of course not," she broke in. "We spend hours and hours every day online, so Mate Match is the perfect place for you to look for love." Then she added, "You write your profile. But Aaron and I will check it before you upload it."

Aaron is Georgia's new boyfriend. All the girls think he is a "real hottie". Whatever that means.

Tuesday 28th of June
11.00 a.m.

Today I sneaked into Mr Scott's office and signed up for Mate Match!

"Joe, you're not the first boy to see me about Mate Match," Mr Scott said. "Not by a long way."

7.00 p.m.

I sat down and wrote my profile. It took me ages, but once it was finished I felt really pleased with it.

'When I've got a girlfriend,' I thought, 'I won't care who knows how I found her.'

7.05 p.m.

Aaron just arrived at our house. He isn't any taller than me and his skin is a bit worse than mine. But he's got a blond streak in his hair and works out at the gym every day. He glides about with such confidence.

'Why can't I ever strut about like I own the place like that?' I thought. No one ever teaches you stuff like gliding and strutting, do they?

7.40 p.m.

I was glowing with pride as I showed Georgia and Aaron my profile. Georgia only read the first couple of lines before she sighed.

"Joe," she sighed. "You've put down here that you love cooking."

"I do," I said. "It's my top hobby. That's why I wrote so much about it."

"And it makes you sound so sweet," Georgia said. "Do you want to be sweet?"

"Well no," I admitted.

"Last weekend I went swimming with dolphins," Aaron said. "You can put that down if you like."

"Brilliant," said Georgia.

"I'm also in a band," Aaron said. "And I think you should be too."

In fact, the two of them rewrote my whole profile from start to finish.

8.25 p.m.

For my profile photo Aaron lent me his white vest and jacket. And I posed with his ukulele.

"That ukulele is different in a good way," Georgia said. "It'll make you look like a real hipster."

"But I can't play it," I said.

"What does that matter?" Georgia asked.

Then Georgia started snapping photos – but she stopped just as fast as she'd started. "Joe, why are you smiling?" she demanded.

"Just to be friendly," I said.

Aaron and Georgia shook their heads in disbelief.

"You never ever smile in pictures, Joey," Aaron said. He didn't smile much in real life, either.

I stared at him. "You called me Joey," I said.

"Yeah," said Aaron, "because I think Joey sounds hotter."

"Much hotter," Georgia agreed.

So I even got a new name. And then I was ready to send myself off to Mate Match.

Wednesday 29th of June

7.10 p.m.

Incredible! Totally incredible.

Mate Match messaged me in less than 24 hours. In under a day, I got a match of my own!

Chapter 3
Making a Match

Wednesday 29th of June

7.20 p.m.

My match was called Tania. I could see from her photo that she's very beautiful with long brown hair and lovely big eyes.

"Joey, you are so cool," she wrote. Which also means I'm hot.

No wonder I couldn't believe it.

8.00 p.m.

Georgia and Aaron couldn't believe it either.

"I just feel so proud," Georgia said. "Aaron and I have made a gorgeous girl fancy you." Then she added, "You'd better let Aaron reply."

"But isn't it better," I asked, "to let Tania get to know *me* a bit now?"

"Do you want a date or not?" Georgia snapped.

Thursday 30th of June

8.30 p.m.

Tania sent me loads more pictures of herself. In some her hair looked curly. In others it didn't. But in all of them she looked beautiful.

"These photos are a diary of my life for you to see," she said.

She's clearly an original thinker.

9.00 p.m.

Tania even sent me a snap of herself first thing in the morning, without any make-up on. Even then she looked incredible.

31

But Georgia snarled. "No make-up – what rubbish. That girl's got mascara and blusher on, for a start."

'Is Georgia a bit jealous of my stunning match?' I thought.

9.15 p.m.

Aaron went out with his band. But Georgia liked my replies.

"They sound exactly like Aaron," she said. "You're learning, Joey."

Friday 1st of July

7.15 p.m.

Shock news. Tania suggested we meet up at Café Pelican on Saturday night. Even Georgia couldn't believe how fast things have moved.

7.40 p.m.

Georgia, Aaron and I had a pre-date meeting. I wanted to give Tania a rose on our first ever date. But Georgia and Aaron weren't keen.

"Creepy," Georgia said.

"Desperate," added Aaron.

"You've got to remember," Georgia said. "You're hot now."

"I do keep forgetting," I admitted.

"And you know how you smile all the time," Georgia said. "Well, don't."

"On first dates," Aaron said. "I never smile more than twice."

"You can be cute, Joey," said Georgia, "but never corny."

"Never, ever corny," Aaron agreed.

It felt as if I they were coaching me for a really tough exam. It felt like a hot date boot camp.

Saturday 2nd of July

5.00 p.m.

Even Mum and Dad started giving me advice.

"Speak up," Mum said.

"And don't be late," added Dad.

"Oh please," I said. "Dating has moved on since your day."

6.50 p.m.

It was really busy when I arrived at Café Pelican.

I didn't recognise anyone from my school. Which was a relief, even if I'd have liked them to see my beautiful date. But they might have been surprised at how different I looked – I was dressed as Aaron's double. And I was sounding like Aaron's double, too. He'd given me a whole load of his stories to tell.

Of course, I'm not really like Aaron at all. In fact, I am a totally different person.

But still, I was on my first ever date.

Chapter 4
First Date

Saturday 2nd of July

7.05 p.m.

Tania was late – but only by five minutes.
But I couldn't help worrying. Had she peeped
through the window and then thought, 'No, I
don't fancy him after all'?

7.20 p.m.

The waitress came over. She didn't look any older than me.

"I'm still waiting," I blurted out.

"I can see that," she said. "I just wondered if you wanted anything now?"

"No, I'll wait until ..." My voice fell away.

"Girls are usually late," she said.

Her voice was kind and she was really pretty, with jet-black hair and pale green eyes.

"Yeah they are," I agreed and then added, "So how are you?"

The waitress looked a bit surprised by the question but then she leaned forward and whispered, "I hate it here actually."

"Why?" I asked.

"Well, they're paying me next to nothing and the woman who runs this place shouts at me all time. I'm only here because I love cooking and they promised ..."

"I love cooking too," I told her.

"Do you really?" the waitress asked. I noticed that her eyes were fixed on me. "So what are your best dishes?"

I was still telling her when Tania glided in. She looked exactly like a model. The waitress melted away.

"Sorry, Joey," Tania said, and she gave me a dazzling smile.

In fact, the sight of her was so dazzling that I forgot I wasn't supposed to smile. I was so incredibly pleased to see her. 'Is this amazing-looking girl really here on a date with me?' I thought.

Tania didn't sit down. She was too busy taking selfies of herself arriving.

"Sorry about this," she said. "But I'm now on five different sites and they'll want to see this."

"You look incredible," I said.

"Thanks, but if I don't get 20 likes in the next half-hour then this picture will be deleted. I'm hoping for 40 likes."

"I'm sure you'll get at least that many," I said. "If not more."

7.40 p.m.

So far Tania had only asked me one question. "Is your band on YouTube?"

Aaron had prepared me an answer for this one. "No," I said. "Not yet, but very soon we will be."

Tania told me that her ambition is to do hair and make-up tutorials on YouTube.

I agreed that her hair was every bit as dazzling as her smile. It would be no surprise if one day it got its own website.

7.52 p.m.

The meal arrived. But Tania didn't eat any of it. She was too busy taking photos of it.

"I like to make people jealous," she said with a grin.

I wanted to yell out, "Just eat it." After all, it was the most expensive meal on the menu. And she hardly touched a morsel.

8.05 p.m.

I asked Tania how many selfies she takes a day.

"Only around 50," she replied. "But I know girls who upload around 200 a day." She paused to check her face in a little mirror. "Now that's just showing off," she said. "And I hate vain people."

8.23 p.m.

Tania told me that I was the sixth person she'd met on Mate Match. I wasn't as upset as I'd expected. I felt proud to be sitting opposite her. But I was also quite bored.

8.40 p.m.

Tania asked me some more about my band. That was all she seemed interested in.

In the end I said, "In fact, I've just been chucked out of the band."

Her mouth opened wide in horror.

"But why, Joey?" she cried.

"Because I'm total rubbish and can't play a note," I said.

"But can I still have a picture with your ukulele?" she demanded.

"Sorry, I just sold it," I said. "And by the way I'm not even called Joey. My real name is Joe."

8.50 p.m.

Tania didn't stay long after all that shocking news. I was kind of relieved. Pretending to be hot really took it out of me. But I decided not to go home just yet. I decided just to sit there, drink a coffee and relax a bit.

9.00 p.m.

My waitress appeared at my table, but she wasn't wearing her uniform any more.

I stared at her. "You've changed."

"Well spotted," she said with a grin.

"You've walked out then?" I said.

"I couldn't stand it here another second," she said. "What about your ..."

"Gone home early," I told her.

She nodded.

"I'm Joe by the way," I said.

"I'm Emily."

'Wow!' I thought. 'A girl's told me her name. That's a first.'

"I don't suppose," I asked, "that you'd like to have a coffee with me?"

She fixed her green eyes on me again.

"Do you know what, I think I would," she said.

10.15 p.m.

Aaron and Georgia were waiting for me when I got home.

"You're late," Georgia said, "which is a really good sign."

I treated them to a mysterious smile.

"So how did it go?" Georgia asked. "And are you going to see her again?"

At that moment a message lit up my phone.

I had a great time and I'd love to see you again. Emily.

I showed the message to Aaron and Georgia.

"What a player," Aaron began, but then he stopped. "I thought her name was Tania?"

"Her name *is* Tania," Georgia said. "Who on earth is Emily?"

"Emily is the waitress," I said.

"The waitress?" Aaron and Georgia echoed together.

"That's right." I grinned. "I've got a lot to tell you."

Our books are tested
for children and young people by
children and young people.

Thanks to everyone who consulted on
a manuscript for their time and effort in
helping us to make our books better
for our readers.

PETE JOHNSON has written lots of laugh-out-loud fiction including ...

Hero

Laugh-out-loud fun from the 'devastatingly f[unny] Pete Johnson'
The Sunday Times

Six Hours

Laugh-out-loud fun from the 'devastatingly funny Pete Johnson'
The Sunday Times

Laugh-out-loud fun from the
"devastatingly funny Pete Johnson"
The Sunday Times

Awesome

Pete Johnson

www.barringtonstoke.co.uk